Sweet Tooth

WRITTEN BY
Michael Lashley

ILLUSTRATED BY
Ana Rankovic

What a risk to take
with chocolate cake.
Cookies would be so plain.
Ice cream would be so tame.
Candy would be so lame.
Nothing would taste the same!

I'll brush you everyday.
I'll let you have your delicious way.

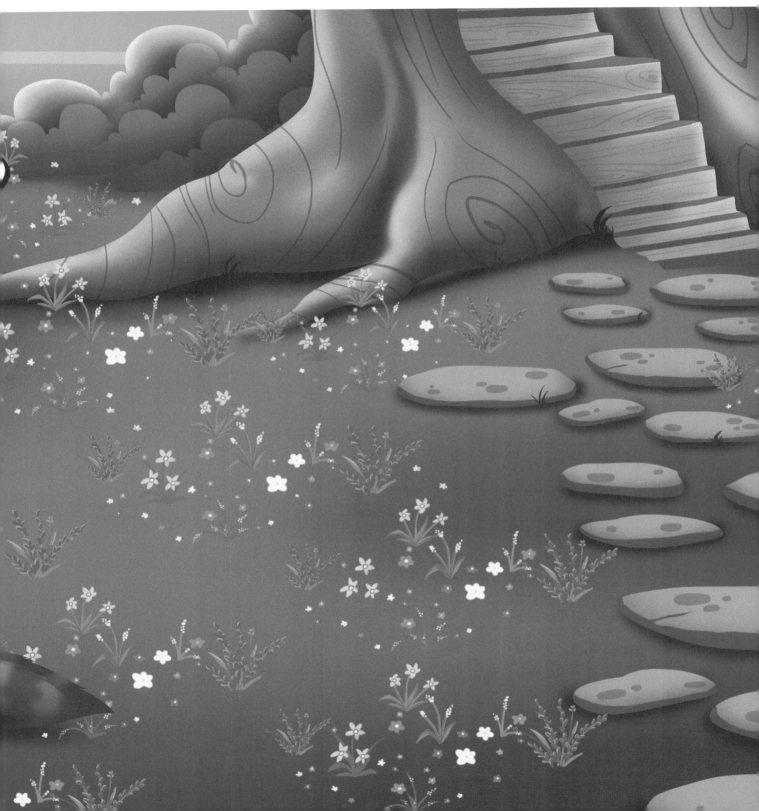

Or, just maybe...

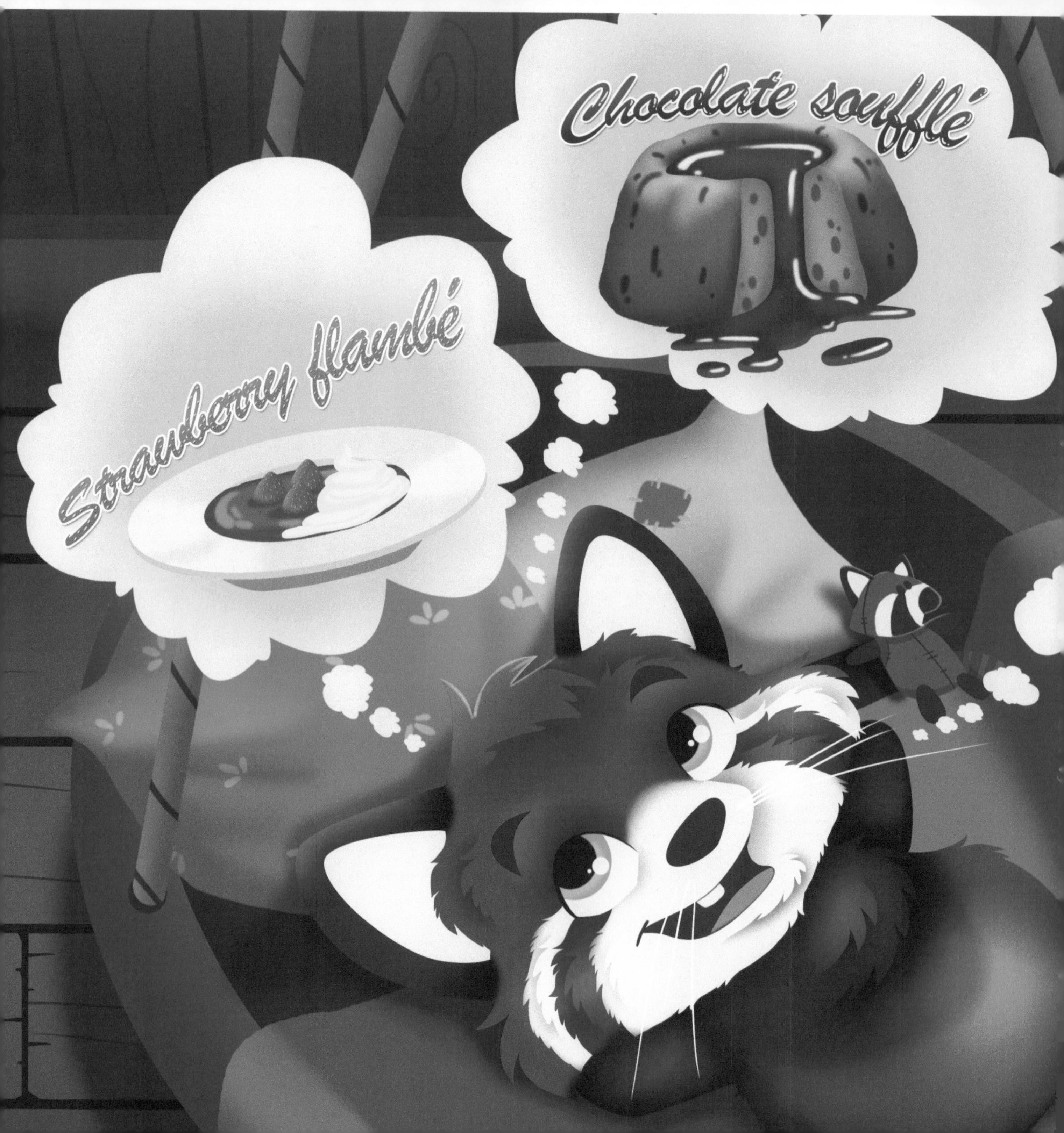
Chocolate soufflé
Strawberry flambé

Creme Brûlée

I could taste things I've never tasted before, like Creme Brûlée, chocolate soufflé, or strawberry flambé.

Where's my sweet tooth?
It's down the drain!

PONGA PUBLISHING COMPANY

Ponga: Sweet Tooth Copyright © 2020 by Michael Lashley

For information address Ponga Publishing,
107 Pacolet Trail. Piedmont, SC 29673
www.pongabooks.com

ISBN 978-1-735-28330-2 (Hardcover)

First Edition